D0605593

DEDICATION

Uriel Dana is a redheaded artist.
She's my wife, and a
Fabulous cook.
I mention her here
To give her a cheer,
'Cause she had the idea
For this book.
— G.T.

© 1995 by Gage Taylor.
All rights reserved.

Book design by Joyce Marie Kuchar.
Typeset in Bernhard Modern and Adobe Garamond.
The illustrations in this book were painted in oil.
Printed in Singapore.

Library of Congress Cataloging-in-Publication Data:
Taylor, Gage.
    Bears at work ; a book of bearable jobs / Gage Taylor.
          64 p.   20.4 x 20.4 cm.
    Summary: A rhyming alphabet describes some of the jobs
    that bears can hold, from adventurer to zookeeper.
    ISBN 0-8118-0844-0
    [1. Occupation—Fiction.   2. Bears—Fiction.   3. Alphabet.]
    4. Stories in rhyme.   I. Title.
    PZ8.3.T2148Be   1995
    [E]—dc20   94-32764
                                          CIP
                                          AC

Distributed in Canada by Raincoast Books
8680 Cambie Street, Vancouver, B.C. V6P 6M9

10 9 8 7 6 5 4 3 2 1

Chronicle Books
275 Fifth Street, San Francisco, California 94103

Bears at Work

A Book of Bearable Jobs

by Gage Taylor

Chronicle Books San Francisco

Adventurers' work
Can be very exciting,
With travel
To faraway lands.
Sometimes there's danger
From mysterious strangers,
If that's what
The journey demands.

Bakers work hard,
And their days are quite long,
But I think their job sounds
Quite good.
They get to take
Bites of cookies and cake
To make sure it all tastes
Like it should.

Comics sleep late
And they work alone.
They don't have to
Hire a big staff.
But if they're not funny
They don't make much money,
'Cause their job's
To make people laugh.

Dancers work out
To stay in good shape.
They have to be
Nimble and strong
To move with such grace
All over the place,
And end up just
Where they belong.

Egyptologists study
Hieroglyphics and mummies
And tombs
From a long time ago.
What are the odds
That the animal gods
Really lived then,
And stood in a row?

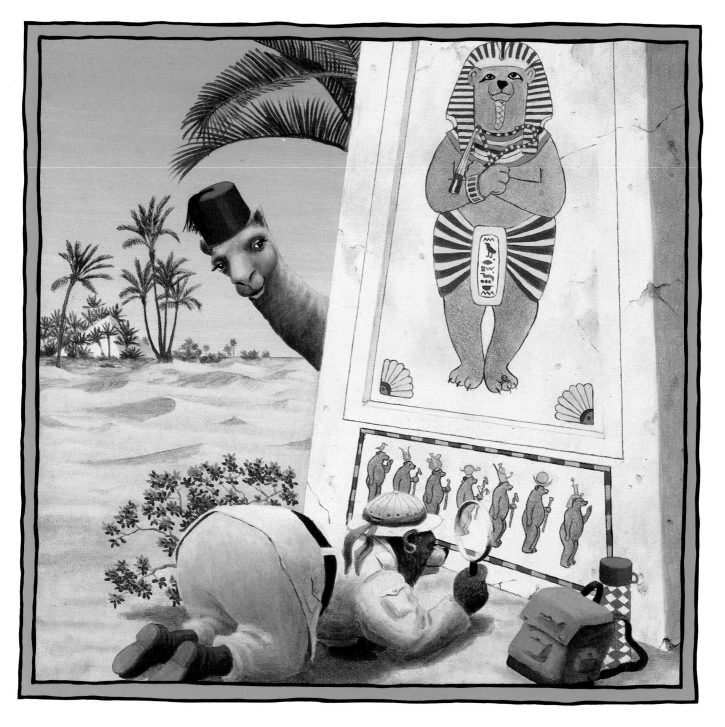

Fortune tellers predict
What life's going to bring,
And sometimes right
Over the phone.
Though having it done
Can sometimes be fun,
The future you make
Is your own.

Golfers have fun,
And they play outside,
But one thing must be
Understood:
If you play it for money
To spend on your honey,
You have to be
Awfully good.

Hypnotherapists take us
Down deep in a trance,
Which requires a
Definite knack.
We go far in the past
To the life we lived last,
Then they
Bring us all the way back.

Interpreters speak
More than one language well.
They deal with some
Tense situations.
They help us cooperate
So we can communicate,
And that's a worthwhile
Occupation.

Jugglers must have
A good sense of timing,
And must concentrate
With great care,
'Cause whether it's cans
Or Chinese silk fans,
It all has to stay
In the air.

Kings get to tell
Everyone what to do
While sitting up there
On the throne.
But if no queen's by his side
In whom to confide,
It's no fun being boss
All alone.

Lifeguards keep an eye
On swimmers who swim
Just a little too far
Out to sea.
They sit in the sun
Watching people have fun.
It seems like
A good job to me.

Musicians can make
What they do look so easy
When we see them
Just sit there and play.
The reason it flows
Is right under your nose:
They practice it
Day after day.

Nannies take care
Of the children at home,
Or take them all out
To the zoo.
When it's time for your nap,
You can sit in her lap,
And she'll tell you
A story or two.

Opera singers dress up
In strange-looking clothes,
And sing just as loud
As they can.
And when they are done,
I'm sure that it's fun,
Hearing all the applause
From their fans.

Painters use color
On canvas or paper
To show us how they
Really feel.
Sometimes it's funny,
Or drippy and runny,
And sometimes it looks
Almost real.

Quarterbacks' work can
Bring glamour and fame.
The job has a
Heroic sound.
But sometimes you'll find
They get hit from behind,
And end up flat out
On the ground.

Restaurant critics
Work for a newspaper,
Or maybe a food
Magazine.
They sample the dinners,
Then report on the winners.
That's the best job I
Ever have seen.

Sculptors make statues
That stand in the park,
Or statues that stand
In the Louvre.
A bit of advice—
You'd better think twice.
Don't make them too
Heavy to move.

Thespians are actors
Who get to pretend
In a movie or
In a play.
And if they work hard
(or win an award),
They get paid to pretend
Every day.

Umpires enforce
The rules of the game.
He's someone you don't
Want to cross.
If he says you're out,
You'd better not shout.
In the end, he's the one
Who is boss.

Ventriloquists talk
Without moving their lips.
If you watch him,
I think you'll agree:
The voice seems to come
Approximately from
The dummy that sits
On his knee.

Weathermen tell us
Just what to expect,
Like a storm that might come
In the night.
They believe it sincerely
And explain it so clearly.
Sometimes they've
Even been right.

Xylophone makers
Build instruments from
Wooden tubes that are
Hollow and round.
And when one is played
With the sticks that they made,
It makes
An incredible sound.

Yoga teachers sit
In a lotus position,
And wait for the noise
To subside.
Their job's to teach
All their students to reach
That calm place
We all have inside.

Zookeepers get to
Take care of the animals,
Though some must be kept
In a cage.
There's been some objection,
But it's for their protection.
They're still at a
Primitive stage.

FAMILIUS HUMANUS